Buying Heifers

Colorado Cowboy Series
Book 4

Dave and Pat Sargent are longtime residents of Prairie Grove, Arkansas. Dave, a fourth-generation dairy farmer, began writing in early December of 1990. Pat, a former teacher, began writing in the fourth grade. They enjoy the outdoors and have a real love for animals.

Buying Heifers

Colorado Cowboy Series
Book 4

Dave and Pat Sargent

Illustrated by Jane Lenoir

Ozark Publishing, Inc.
P.O. Box 228
Prairie Grove, AR 72753

Cataloging-in-Publication Data

Sargent, Dave, 1941–
    Buying heifers / by Dave and Pat Sargent ;
illustrated by Jane Lenoir. —Prairie Grove, AR :
Ozark Publishing, c2005.
        p. cm.   (Colorado cowboy series ; 4)

    "Don't give up"—Cover.
    SUMMARY: Life on the Hatchet Ranch
gets exciting when some mad mama pigs
attack a cowboy who catches a baby pig by
the tail! And when the boys saddle up and
ride to Colorado to bring back three hundred
heifers the boss has purchased, things begin
happening. Some good. Some bad.
        ISBN 1-59381-096-2 (hc)
              1-59381-097-0 (pbk)
              1-59381-564-6 (pfb)
        1. Cowboys—Juvenile fiction.
2. Cowgirls—Juvenile fiction.
[1. Cowhands—Fiction.] 1. Sargent, Pat, 1936–
II. Lenoir, Jane, 1950– ill. IV. Title. V. Series:
    PZ7.S243Bu 2005
    [Fic]—dc21   2003099182

Printed in the United States of America

iv

Inspired by

the sleek trim Jersey heifers we raised on our dairy farm. And all the young beef heifers we've seen.

Dedicated to

all kids who live on a farm. And to those involved in F.F.A. projects.

Foreword

Life on the Hatchet Ranch gets exciting when some mad mama pigs attack a cowboy who catches a baby pig by the tail! And when the boys saddle up and ride to Colorado to bring back three hundred heifers the boss has purchased, things begin happening. Some good. Some bad.

Contents

If you would like to have the authors of the Colorado Cowboy Series visit your school, free of charge, call either of these numbers: 1-800-321-5671 or 1-800-960-3876.

One

Mad Mama Pigs!

The Colorado sky was clear and blue. "Hmm," Sam Aldred thought. "This is good. Everything looks peaceful."

Sam loped his dun horse toward the Hatchet Ranch. He smiled and patted the dun on his neck.

"It feels good to be home again, Monty," he said.

The dun nickered softly. Sam reined him to a halt at the barn.

All of a sudden a pig squealed. Then he heard a lot of pigs squealing.

"What's going on? It sounds like some of the mama pigs are upset about something," Sam muttered.

And that's when he heard all of the cowhands laughing like crazy. The laughter was evidently coming from the pig pen that was out behind the barn.

"I wonder what those cowhands are up to. Sounds like they're having a little too much fun to be working," he said with eyebrows raised and a quizzical look on his face.

When Sam rounded the corner of the barn, he came to a sudden stop. What he saw would make anyone in their right mind, laugh.

A cowhand was sitting on the top rail of the fence. And on the ground under him, mad Mama pigs were oinking and biting at his boots!

"Buck!" Sam yelled "What did you do to make those pigs so mad? Get out of their pen!"

"He can't get down, Boss," Luke chuckled. "Those mad mama's will eat him alive!"

The noise from the pigs grew louder. The cowboys laughed harder.

"Old Buck can't sit there on top of that fence all day!" Sam yelled. "Get some feed! Maybe it'll take their minds off that crazy cowboy."

One of the cowhands ran to get some feed.

"What did Buck do to make them so mad?" Sam asked.

"He caught one of the babies by the tail," Luke said. "And when it squealed, all of the mama's got mad."

The cowhand returned with a bucket of skim milk. He poured it into the trough. The pigs ran to the trough to eat. And a moment later, the mamas and babies were quiet and content with the skim milk.

Sam grinned. "By doggies, I'm glad that noise stopped," he said, with a nod of his head. "Buck, I hope you learned a lesson about pigs."

"I did, Boss," Buck said. "I'm a cattle wrangler. Not a pig herder."

"You've been gone about two weeks, Boss," Luke said. "Did you find some good heifers to buy?"

"I sure did," Sam said. "There's a big Hereford ranch in southeast Colorado. I made a deal for three hundred head."

"Are they bringing them to us?" Luke asked. "That's a long trek from here, Boss."

"Nope. It's range delivery," Sam said. "I'll take seven or eight cowboys with me. You'll stay here and be in charge of things while we're gone."

"Sounds good to me," Luke smiled. "I reckon you'll leave Buck here to feed the pigs?"

"I think Buck better ride with me," Sam chuckled. "Maybe I can keep him out of trouble."

That night the cowboys sat down to supper.

"Get your fill of good food, Boys," Sam grinned. "The vittles we'll have on the trail won't be this hot or good."

One of the cowboys looked at Luke.

"Did you hear that?" he asked. "No hot biscuits until we get back."

The cowhands laughed.

"That's bad for Luke. He can't get up in the morning without a hot biscuit waiting for him," another chuckled.

"Humph," Luke fussed. "I may be getting old, and I do like my hot biscuits, so I'm staying here. The boss needs a feller with good sense to take care of you loco cowboys."

Sam smiled. "Ron, I want you, Buck, and five other riders to go with me. It's a long trek there and back. The Hereford Ranch is on the eastern plains of Colorado. And storms come up fast out there. We'll go east along the Arkansas River."

"When do we leave, Boss?" Ron asked.

"In the morning," Sam said. "We'll ride from daylight to dark. We should get there in five days."

Luke grinned and winked.

"Don't you worry about a thing here, Boss," he said. "I'll take care of the Hatchet and the hot biscuits."

Two

Stampede!

At dawn the next morning, Sam and the cowhands left the ranch. Sam nudged his dun into a running walk. And throughout the daylight hours, the cowboys kept that pace for the entire five day trek.

At noon on the fifth day, Sam nudged his horse into a lope.

"There's the main ranch house," he said. "It's time to go to work."

Buck groaned.

"What's the matter with you, Buck?" Sam asked.

"I've been riding in a trot for five days," he said. "My backside has blisters."

The cowboys laughed.

Ron said, "You'll be all right, Buck. Maybe that saddle will break them on the way home."

"You're a lot of help," Buck grumbled.

"Maybe this ranch has some pigs," Sam chuckled. "While we gather cattle, you can sort the pigs."

"Humph," Buck snorted. "I'd rather have blisters."

Two days later, Sam and the boys had gathered all three hundred head of heifers.

Sam pointed to two of the young heifers. They were snorting and their eyes looked wild. Their heads were high in the air.

"Those two are trouble," he said. "They're spooky. Crazy cattle like that could start a stampede."

The cowboys agreed.

"Ron, I'll ride point. You and Buck ride on each side of the herd. The rest of you fellers push them from behind. Get them strung out along the trail."

For three days, the cattle drive was quiet and calm. On the third night, they bedded down beside the Arkansas River.

"Who wants to take first watch over the herd?" Sam asked.

Buck stood up. "I will, Boss," he said. "I can't sit down very good anyway."

Sam grinned and said, "Okay, Buck. You stay with the herd until midnight. Then I'll take over."

Two hours later, everyone was asleep but Buck. He slowly rode his horse around the quiet herd of heifers. The night was peaceful and quiet. But a dark cloud was moving swiftly toward them.

Without warning, a sudden bolt of lightning struck a tree nearby. When thunder shook the ground, the two spooky heifers jumped up. They ran through the herd. Seconds later, cattle were bawling and running.

When Sam heard the thunder, he leaped to his feet.

"Wake up, Boys! We may have a stampede on our hands!" he yelled.

The men quickly saddled their horses. Sam kicked his horse into a dead run. Soon rain began to fall and lightning lit up the sky. Sam pushed his horse to run faster. He saw Buck leaned over the neck of his running horse. The herd was scared, running blindly through the night. Sam felt something hard hit him. "Oh no," he groaned. "Hail!" He looked around. His cowboys were riding with him.

"Turn the heifers away from the river!" he yelled. "Hurry! That river can flood real fast. This herd could drown if we don't turn them back."

Sam felt his horse flinch as hail pelted him. "Come on, Monty," he said in an urgent voice. "We can do this! Just get ahead of them."

The dun horse raced through the storm. When another lightning bolt lit up the land, Sam saw a body sprawled on the ground. The herd was running straight toward it. He reined Monty toward the still form.

"Buck," he gasped.

Buck staggered to his feet. Sam reined his horse in front of the herd and turned him toward the cowboy. He reached down and grabbed Buck and pulled him up behind the saddle.

Sam reined his horse to the right. The herd ran past. The other cowboys raced ahead of them.

Sam reined his horse to a halt and helped Buck off. The injured cowboy fell onto the muddy ground.

"What happened, Buck?" Sam asked.

"One of those spooky heifers ran into my horse. It scared him and he threw me," Buck gasped. "I think my leg's broken."

Then Sam saw blood running down Buck's face. "Did you get cut?" he asked.

"My horse ran over me," Buck said. "He kicked me in the head."

Sam dragged the hurt cowboy beneath a tree. He pulled the saddle and blanket off his horse and covered Buck with the saddle blanket.

"Just rest, Buck," Sam said. "The storm is about over. We'll get you some help. Just rest for a while."

Three

The Trail Drive Home

By dawn the next morning, the storm was over. Sam looked at Buck. The cut on his head had stopped bleeding. His eye was black. And his leg was broken. But the injured cowboy was sleeping peacefully. Sam slowly stood up. He caught his horse and jumped on him bareback.

"Lets go find the other hands and the herd, Monty," he whispered.

A short time later, he found them. The cowboys were tired, wet, and hungry. The heifers were quiet.

"We were getting ready to look for you, Boss," Ron said. "Are you okay?"

"Yeah," Sam said.

"We've searched for Buck, but we've not seen him, Boss," Ron said. "We did find his horse."

Sam nodded. "Buck's hurt bad, Boys," he said. "He was kicked in the head. And his leg is broken. I'm going to need two of you to take him to a doctor."

As they followed Sam back to where he had left Buck, Ron said, "I'll go, Boss."

"No," Sam said. "We're going to be three men short in driving this herd home. I need you to help me with the cattle drive. I know you all are tired. But I need two other fellers to take Buck to a nearby town."

"I'll be fine, Boss," Buck said. "I can ride to the doc by myself. You're gonna need these boys for the trail drive."

"No, I don't," Sam said. "Those heifers are plumb tuckered out from running last night. I don't think we'll have any trouble out of them."

The boys put Buck on a horse. A cowboy rode on each side of him.

"Buck," Sam called. "We'll see you at the ranch later. Now you boys take it easy with him."

A short time later, the heifers were once again strung out along the trail. A cowboy rode on each side of the herd. Sam rode point. And two cowhands pushed them slowly from the back of the herd. The two spooky heifers were in the lead. But they were much calmer than they had been the day before.

"I think we broke those two loco heifers," Ron chuckled.

"It looks like it," Sam agreed.

"We may have them broke to ride before we get home."

The cowboys all laughed. They were tired, hungry, and dirty, but proud of their night's work.

That night they ate cold biscuits and beef jerky beside a campfire. Ron stood watch over the cattle until midnight. Then Sam took his place. It was a peaceful, restful night.

Ten days later, the cowboys and three hundred head of heifers arrived at the Hatchet Ranch. Sam saw Luke loping his horse toward them. He was waving his hat in the air.

"Welcome home, Boss," Luke shouted.

"Thanks, Luke," Sam grinned. "It's sure good to be back."

Luke looked at the herd for a moment. "We have the pens and feed all ready for this bunch of heifers. And they are just like you said, Boss. They are mighty fine ones."

"Is everything okay here?" Sam asked.

"Not a bit of trouble, Boss," Luke grinned.

All of a sudden Sam looked serious.

"Did Buck and the other two cowhands make it back, Luke?"

"They sure did, Boss," he said. Then he glared at Sam. "I've thought about sending them back to eastern Colorado. That ornery old Buck just can't stay out of trouble!"

"What happened?" Sam asked.

"One of the cowhands was in the pig pen," Luke said. "Buck was hobbling around with his crutch. I'll be doggone if he didn't grab a baby pig by the tail again!"

"Uh oh," Sam said. "And did that cowhand get bit by a mad pig?"

"Nope," Luke said. "And I was that cowhand, Boss. I sat on top of that fence until after dark that night!"

Sam and the cowboys whooped and hollered and laughed.

Four

Cowboy Facts

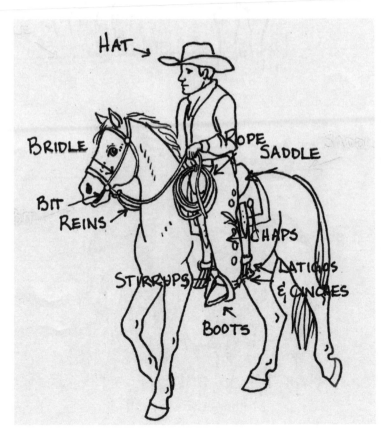

Heifer

Mother cow with calf